Kitty Cat, Kitty Cat,

Are You Going to Sleep?

BY Bill Martin Jr and Michael Sampson

ILLUSTRATED BY Laura J. Bryant

SCHOLASTIC INC.

No part of this publication may be reproduced, stored in a retrieval system, or transmitted in any form or by any means, electronic, mechanical, photocopying, recording, or otherwise, without written permission of the publisher.
For information regarding permission, write to Amazon Children's Publishing, PO Box 400818, Las Vegas, NV 89149.

ISBN 978-0-545-51961-8

Text copyright © 2011 by Michael Sampson and Bill Martin Jr.
Illustrations copyright © 2011 by Laura J. Bryant.
All rights reserved. Published by Scholastic Inc., 557 Broadway, New York, NY 10012, by arrangement with Amazon Children's Publishing.
SCHOLASTIC and associated logos are trademarks and/or registered trademarks of Scholastic Inc.

12 11 10 9 8 7 6 5 4 3 2 1   12 13 14 15 16 17/0

Printed in the U.S.A.   40

First Scholastic printing, October 2012

The text of this book is set in Classical Garamond.
The illustrations are rendered in watercolor paints and colored pencils on Strathmore paper.
Book design by Anahid Hamparian
Editor: Margery Cuyler

To Michelle
—M.S.

To Andy and Andria
—L.J.B.

"**Kitty Cat, Kitty Cat,**
the day is almost done."

"Not yet, Mother,
I still can see the sun."

"Kitty Cat, Kitty Cat,
I am calling you."

"I know, Mother,
let's play peekaboo!"

"Kitty Cat, Kitty Cat,
are you in the tub?"

"Not yet, Mother,
I do not like to scrub."

"Kitty Cat, Kitty Cat,
did you wash your face?"

"Not yet, Mother,
I'm in outer space."

"Kitty Cat, Kitty Cat,
put on your night clothes."

"Not yet, Mother,
I'm playing with my toes."

"Kitty Cat, Kitty Cat,
have you brushed your teeth?"

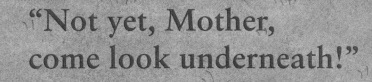

"Not yet, Mother,
come look underneath!"

"Kitty Cat, Kitty Cat,
it's time to read a book."

"Okay, Mother,
I know where to look."

"Kitty Cat, Kitty cat,
lay down your sleepy head."

"Okay, Mother,
I guess it's time for bed."

"Kitty Cat, Kitty Cat,
you've finally closed your eyes."

"That's right, Mother,
time for lullabies."

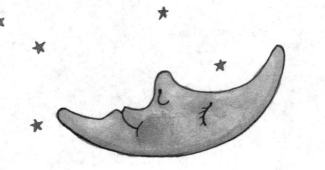

"Kitty Cat, Kitty Cat,
I'm turning out the light."

"Good night, Mother,
I will sleep *sooo* tight."